LITTLE HOUSES

By Kevin Henkes

Illustrated by Laura Dronzek

GREENWILLOW BOOKS

An Imprint of HarperCollinsPublishers

Little Houses
Text copyright © 2022 by Kevin Henkes;
illustrations copyright © 2022 by Laura Dronzek
All rights reserved. Manufactured in Italy.
For information address HarperCollins Children's Books,
a division of HarperCollins Publishers,
195 Broadway, New York, NY 10007.
www.harpercollinschildrens.com

Acrylic paints were used to prepare the full-color art.
The text type is 25-point Carre Noir Pro.

Library of Congress Cataloging-in-Publication Data is available.

ISBN 9780062965721 (hardback) | ISBN 9780062965738 (lib. bdg.)

22 23 24 25 26 RTLO 10 9 8 7 6 5 4 3 2 1
First Edition

Greenwillow Books

For Will and Clara

When I visit my grandparents at the beach,
we stay in a little house.
It is so close to the water,
you can hear the waves.

Sometimes I think someone
is calling me.
But it's just the waves
coming in, going out.
A whisper or a roar.
I run up and down to meet them.

Every morning we look for shells.

We almost always find something good.

We only keep the ones that are empty.

Grandma reminds me that the shells
are little houses.
And that gets me thinking.

Thinking of thin pale walls

of pink or gray,

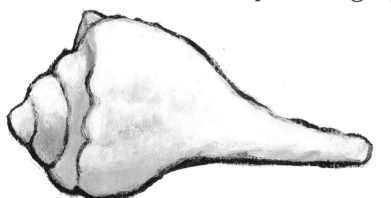

white or white,

shiny or dull.

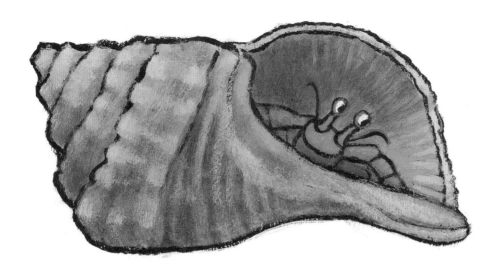

A rounded orange room

or one with brown spots

like freckles.

But who lived here?

Where is it now?

Is its ghost still inside

the curved walls?

Is that the sound in a shell?

Is that the tiny ghost I hear?

We look for empty little houses all morning.

Over the sound of the waves, I hear Grandma say,

". . . things we cannot see."

I don't know what she's talking about,

but I nod anyway and wonder about

all the things that might be under the water.

Fish as big as cars,

creatures whose names I don't know,

lost toys,

lost coins,

lots of lost things

that were cried over.

Things that might turn up one day,

rolling onto the shore.

Maybe just a piece of something to show everyone.

"Beautiful, beautiful. Just beautiful,"
Grandpa always says.
He also says, "The world is so big
and there is so much to know.
And someday you'll know it all."
We both smile.

I *would* like to know it all.

I'd like to know how far each shell has traveled

and how old the rocks and stones are.

I'd like to know

how deep the water is at its very deepest part

and how it can be blue and gray and green
and silver and white and black, all at the same time.

I'd like to know

what a pelican thinks of a sandpiper

and if a snowy egret has ever seen snow.

So right now, I'll walk up and down
the beach
looking for little houses
and thinking about everything I don't know.

But one thing I *do* know
is that I will take some little houses
back to *my* house,
where they'll sit on the shelf
in my bedroom.
I'll put my favorite
in a special place.

A house
in a house
in the world.